S0-BAD-407

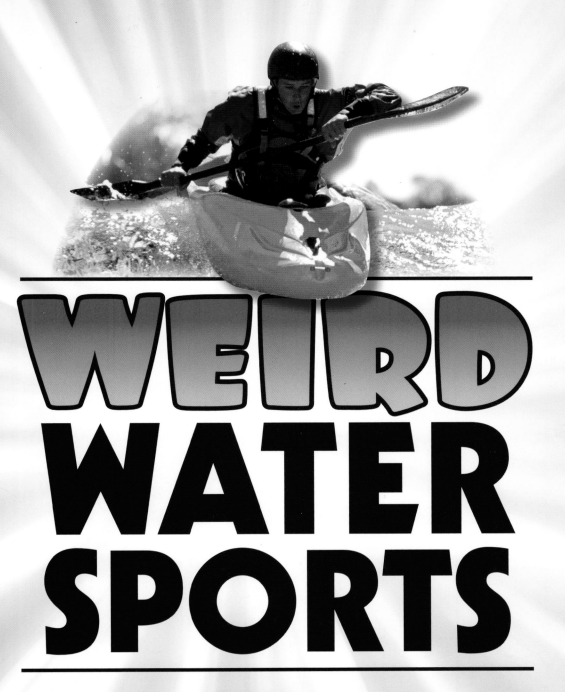

WEIRD
WATER
SPORTS

By K.C. Kelley

The Child's World

Published by The Child's World®
1980 Lookout Drive
Mankato, MN 56003-1705
800-599-READ
www.childsworld.com

The Child's World®: Mary Berendes, Publishing Director
The Design Lab: Design and production

Photo credits
Cover: iStock (top and right); Getty Images (left)
Interior: AP/Wide World: 9; ASCE/Phil Klein: 17;
dreamstime.com: 12, 18, Getty Images: 6, 10, 22;
iStock: 5, 21; Catfish Sutton: 14

Library of Congress Cataloging-in-Publication Data
Kelley, K. C.
  Weird water sports / by K.C. Kelley.
    p. cm.
  Includes bibliographical references and index.
  ISBN 978-1-60954-380-8 (library reinforced: alk. paper)
  1. Aquatic sports—Juvenile literature. I. Title.
  GV770.5.K45 2011
  797—dc22   2010044028

Printed in the United States of America
Mankato, Minnesota
December, 2010
PA02070

Above: Ever snorkeled in a bog? This guy has; read more on page 6.

For more information about the photo on page 1, turn to page 12.

TABLE OF CONTENTS

*Water fun for everyone! Dive into this
great collection of weird water sports!*

Water and Weirdness

Why does being wet make people act so oddly? Maybe it's the freedom of floating. Maybe it's because they think they're fish. Maybe they just like splashing. Whatever the reason, people do a lot of weird water sports. Swimmers, skiers, riders, and divers . . . last one into the water is a rotten egg!

Is he jumping in for underwater hockey? Is he going noodling? He's going to have fun, no matter what!

5

SPLISH SPLASH!

The world championships are held in Waen Rhydd, Wales. Believe it or not, you say that "wine reeth." The 2010 winner was Conor Murphy in a time of 1 minute, 42 seconds.

Along with a snorkel, goggles or a face mask are a must for this sport!

Swimming with Leeches

Most people swim in a pool, a lake, or the ocean. Then there are the folks who swim in bogs. A bog is a wetland, sort of like a swamp—but with more mud and less water. In Wales, a part of Great Britain, people actually swim in one bog. The annual World Bog Snorkeling Championships are held there each summer. A narrow path is dug in a bog. Swimmers plunge in and splash to the end of the 60-yard (55-meter) course. Then it's time to pick off the **leeches**, bugs, and slugs that climbed on for the ride!

Slime on My Pedals!

Snorkeling is not the only fun they have in Wales. After the snorkelers are out of the bog, it's time to bring in the bikes! The World Mountain Bike Bog-Racing Championships are held in a very un-bike-friendly place. Riders wear helmets in case of a crash . . . and snorkels in case of a splash. The bikes carry weights so they stay down. The rider does all the work, however . . . and gets really, really wet.

Biking in a bog takes strong legs . . . and the ability to hold your breath!

To make sure that the tires don't make the bike float, they are filled with water!

SPLISH SPLASH!

In 2010, a team from the University of Florida won the U.S. national championship!

Players wear gloves on their hands as protection against swinging sticks.

Face-Off with Flippers

What do you call an ice hockey game on a really, really hot day? Underwater hockey! That may be a joke, but the game of underwater hockey isn't—people really do play this sport! Wearing swim fins, snorkels, and masks, two teams knock around a weighted **puck**. Players come up for air as often as they need to. Still, being able to hold your breath is a good underwater hockey skill. The players swing a short stick with one hand. They aim for goals at either end of a pool. It's more popular in Europe than America, but many U.S. colleges have teams.

A Long, Wet Way Down

Kayaking can be a quiet way to paddle down a calm stream. You move along with the water. You check out the wildlife and the beautiful trees. And then you plunge off the edge of a giant waterfall! Well, you only do that last part if you're one of the folks who do waterfall kayaking. These **daredevils** paddle down a river . . . and then down a waterfall! The idea is to land in the pool at the bottom and keep paddling.

Waterfall kayakers wear helmets, life jackets, and other safety gear.

SPLISH SPLASH!

The world record for the highest waterfall successfully kayaked is 186 feet (57 m). Tyler Bradt made it to the bottom of the Palouse Falls in Washington.

SPLISH SPLASH!

Most people call this sport noodling, but the activity is also known as hogging, tickling, graveling, and dogging.

Face-to-face with a huge catfish . . . and no net to help you haul it out!

Who Needs a Fishing Pole?

If someone tells you they're going noodling, they won't need pasta. Noodling is a very strange way to go fishing—with your hands! Noodlers look for shallow pools of freshwater. Large catfish often hang out in the pools. The noodler slowly reaches down and tries to grab the big fish. The idea is to snag the catfish's lip or mouth and haul it up. But the fish doesn't always want to come up! A struggle follows. Catfish can bite and scratch . . . but for noodlers, this sport is worth the effort!

Seriously . . . Those Float?

Take a piece of concrete and put it in the water. What happens? It sinks. Now imagine making a boat out of concrete! Very smart people can make concrete float—and even move in the water! Concrete canoe races are held between colleges. The students are studying design and **engineering**. They use the lessons learned in class to make boats from concrete. They win awards based on design, speed, and how well the boats float!

Once the students make their boat, they change from builders to paddlers . . . and race!

SPLISH SPLASH!

The most famous barefoot water-skier was "Banana" George Blair of Florida. He was skiing on his feet well into his 90s!

Barefoot water-skiers like this athlete need balance and great timing to stay up.

No Skis Needed!

Water-skiing is not a weird sport. Millions of people have tried it. Some people can even do amazing tricks, such as jumping off ramps and doing flips. Such skiers use one or two skis. However, another group of skiers leaves their skis in the boat—and goes barefoot! Somehow, they balance on one or two bare feet as the boat pulls them through the water. Skilled barefoot skiers can go backward or forward!

Hang Ten . . . No Sharks!

To go surfing, you need two things: a surfboard and waves. Most surfers find their waves in the ocean. But some bold surfers find waves on rivers! These waves are not moving waves like you see at the beach. These rolling waters stay in one place as a fast-moving river flows over a bump in the riverbed. River surfers get up on a board on these waves. They can ride for a long time, since the wave doesn't "break." The sport started on German rivers. It has spread to Canada, Hawaii, and the northwest U.S.

A wetsuit, a surfboard, and great balance are needed to hold your spot while river surfing.

SPLISH SPLASH!

The hottest water sport around is stand-up paddle-boarding. So it's no surprise that stand-up river paddle-boarding is getting popular, too!

21

SPLISH SPLASH!

In 2010, a woman named Barbara Bailey was named the belly-flopping queen of the Redneck Games in Georgia. She flopped wearing a red-white-and-blue dress!

This diver in overalls sent mud flying over all of the spectators!

SPLOOSH!

The last weird water sport is the easiest of the
bunch. Fill a large, shallow pool with mud.
Then flop in! That's exactly what mud-pit
belly flopping is. At hot summer events in the
southern U.S., mud-pit belly flopping draws a
big crowd. Lots of floppers are ready to show off
their style. Splash after splash, they are judged
for how much water they send up and how they
look doing it. Mud-pit belly flopping is fun
(and a big mess) for all ages!

Glossary

daredevils—people who take dangerous chances while doing sports or performing stunts

engineering—the study of how things are built or put together

leeches—types of worms that have teeth or suckers to hold onto prey (or skin!)

puck—a flat-sided round disk used in hockey

Web Sites

For links to learn more about weird sports: **childsworld.com/links**

Note to Parents, Teachers, and Librarians: We routinely verify our Web links to make sure they are safe and active sites. So encourage your readers to check them out!

Index